The Camel That Got Away

In October 2003 some very unusual camels appeared on the streets of Dubai. The **Camel Caravan** was a public art project produced by ArtWorks LLC. Not only was it lots of fun, it also raised large sums of money for children's charities and funding for the arts in Dubai. Everybody loved the camels in their brightly painted costumes.

The Emirates Banker was designed and painted by the students of Latifa College, and became an extremely popular character throughout Dubai. When he mysteriously vanished, newspapers featured his picture, radio stations asked for information and posted a reward for his return, but he was never seen again. A replica now stands outside the headquarters of Emirates Bank.

This is the story of **The Camel That Got Away.**

The first edition of this book would not have been possible
without the generous support of Emirates Bank

Published by JERBOA BOOKS
P O Box 333838 Dubai UAE
www.jerboabooks.com
First Edition printed in 2005
Second Edition printed in 2006
ISBN 9948-426-19-3
Copyright © Julia Johnson 2005
Camel Caravan copyright © ArtWorks LLC
Printed in Dubai

THE CAMEL THAT GOT AWAY

by **Julia Johnson**

Illustrations **Una Rawlinson**

Some most unusual camels
   have come into town -
Unlike real camels they're
   not black or white or brown.
I'm sure you will have seen them
   all around Dubai
For their brightly coloured coats
   really catch the eye.

One day they were standing
   on public display,
And this is the story
   of the one that got away!

A real live camel
    was walking quite near,
She stopped and she blinked
    and she said, 'What's here?

I've never seen camels like these before,
    dressed in painted suits,
One got up like a bumble bee,
    another in climbing boots!

Where are you from,
   please tell me do ?
You must have come
   from a colourful zoo!

Perhaps you've stepped out
   of a fairy tale ?
I know! You've been
   to a jumble sale!

Only joking! Err ...
    could you be movie stars?
Do you drive around
    in big flash cars?

Oh wow, Spidey camel,
a real Super Hero,
And Theatricamel dressed
just like a Pierrot!

Why you two look
most awfully arty!
Are you going to a
fancy dress party?'

There were camels with stripes
    and a camel at sea,
And some inscribed
    with calligraphy.
Palm trees covered
    the coat of one,
Another had mirrors
    which gleamed in the sun.

She looked and she looked
    and she looked some more
For she'd never seen camels
    like these before.

One had flags
    all over his back,
And another was painted
    gold and black.
Some wore moons
    and some wore stars,
She thought perhaps
    they'd come from Mars!

'Hey you there,
    dressed in the fancy kimono,
Are you related
    to Yoko Ono?
And are you Swedish -
    that can't be so,
For surely you'd live
    in the ice and snow!'

A Centurion camel
    said importantly,
'Enough of your nonsense,
    now listen to me!

Don't you know
    it's rude to stare?
I really don't know
    how you dare !

Just look at yourself,
    all dull and brown -
Why we are the best-dressed
    camels in town!

We represent many
    different nations,
Languages, cultures
    and celebrations,
Poetry, sports
    and history too,
And we certainly haven't
    escaped from a zoo!

We've been painted by hand
and carefully made,
And here we stand
on public parade.

We're going to be auctioned
for tons of money.
Now off with you,
you're not at all funny!'

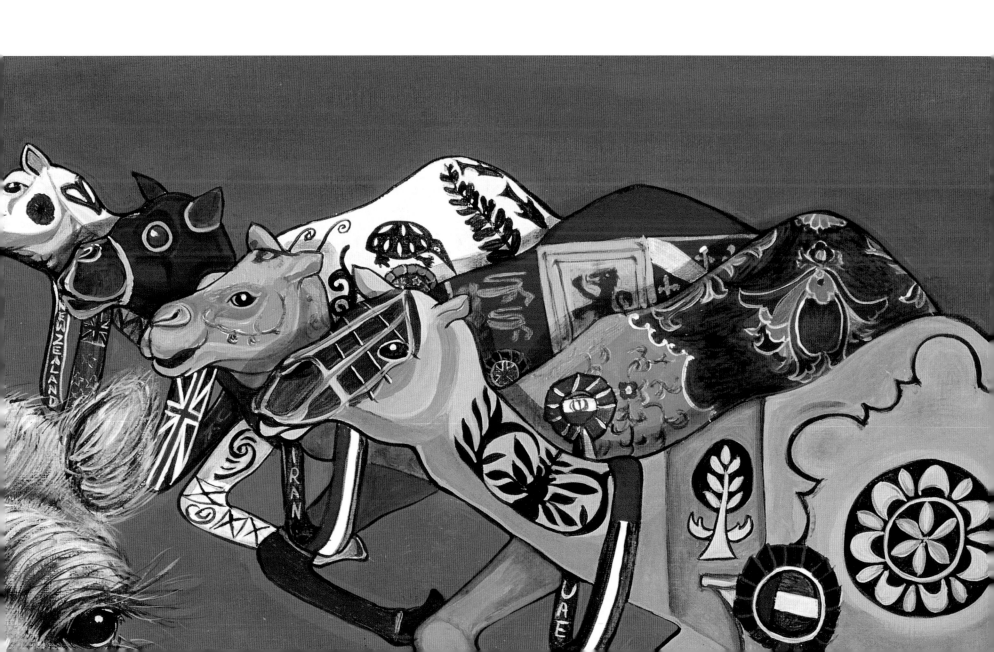

A tear trickled out
of the real camel's eye,
She hung her head
and she gave a big sigh.

But as she began
to walk away
She heard a voice
behind her say,

'Now that's no way
to speak to the lady!
I think your manners
are rather shady.

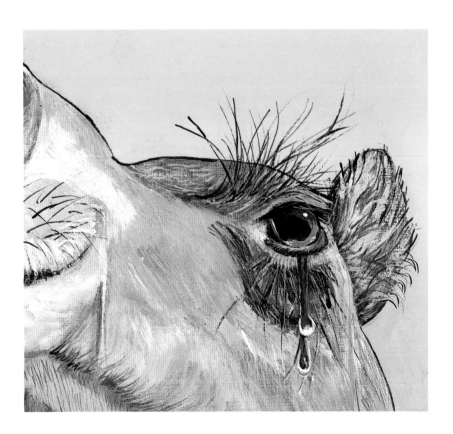

Please, take no notice,
  and come over here,
I would love to talk
  to you, my dear.'

She turned around,
  and his heart missed a beat
For the young lady camel
  was incredibly sweet!
She gazed at him
  and he gazed at her,
And she felt a tingle
  run through her fur!

He was dashingly handsome
    and awfully smart,
And in that moment
    She quite lost her heart.
In his pinstripe suit
    of blue and yellow
And his bowler hat
    he was quite a fellow!

She thought his outfit
    was really natty -
Beside him she felt
    rather drab and tatty.
But he thought her
    quite the prettiest camel,
He asked her name
    and she told him, 'Amal'.
He said, 'I'm called
    the Emirates Banker,'
And added that he
    would like to thank her...

For taking time
    to come over and talk,
And how he would love
    to go for a walk.

'I fear it's impossible
    for me,' he said,
But then an idea
    popped into his head.
'If you will teach me
    what real camels do
Then perhaps I can run
    away with you!'

So she showed him how
real camels run,

How they sit in the sand
always facing the sun.

She showed him, too,
how to close his nose,

How to take a long drink,
and to spread his big toes.

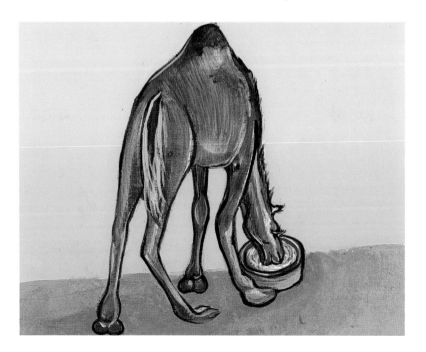

Then he wished and he wished
for all he was worth,
And all of a sudden
a wind shook the earth,
For the Genie camel
was listening well
And under his breath
he had muttered a spell.

Then a whip of sand
spun this way and that,
And our camel, he shouted,
'There goes my hat!'

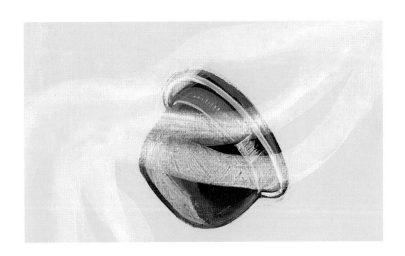

But he gave not a fig,
   he did not care
As away he was whirled
   through the dusty air.
In the blink of an eye
   he had lost his suit,
His monocle, his briefcase
   and his socks to boot!

He went on spinning
   till he felt quite dizzy,
His head was aching,
   his knees went fizzy!

And when at last
   he dropped to the ground
He staggered a bit,
   then he looked around

And there was Amal
   standing under a tree -
She was waiting for him,
   it was plain to see!

So now you know the story
    of the one that got away -
He lives in the desert,
    and that's where he wants to stay.
But when you see a camel,
    if you find when you look
A bit of blue in his coat,
    he's the one from this book!

Julia has always enjoyed storytelling, performing and writing. She has appeared on stage, television and radio in the UK and in Dubai, has toured Theatre-in-Education productions to schools, and recorded many audio books. She first came to Dubai in 1975, and finds the Arabian Peninsula a great source of inspiration.

Julia also enjoys theatre, travel, swimming and diving. This is her eighth book, and her first with Jerboa Books LLC.

Una Rawlinson is an illustrator, painter, muralist and mosaic artist. She has fulfilled a variety of commissions ranging from murals for kindergartens to mosaics for restaurants. She has an honours degree in Art History and Architecture.

Una has spent most of her time in Hong Kong but now lives in Dubai with her husband and daughter.

This is her first children's book.